For Christy, who believed. – V.B.

To my parents, Joe and Carlene, who
have always believed in me. – W.J.

Text copyright © 2020 by Viola Butler
Illustrations copyright © 2020 by Ward Jenkins

ISBN 978-1-948898-01-0

Library of Congress Control Number: 2019952151

Published by FEEDING MINDS PRESS, Washington, D.C.
Book design by Mary A. Burns   Edited by Emma D. Dryden

Printed in the United States of America
10 9 8 7 6 5 4 3 2

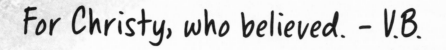

TALES of the DAIRY GODMOTHER
CHUCK'S ICE CREAM WISH

By Viola Butler   Illustrated by Ward Jenkins

ICE CREAM TIME!

FEEDING MINDS PRESS
American Farm Bureau Foundation for Agriculture®

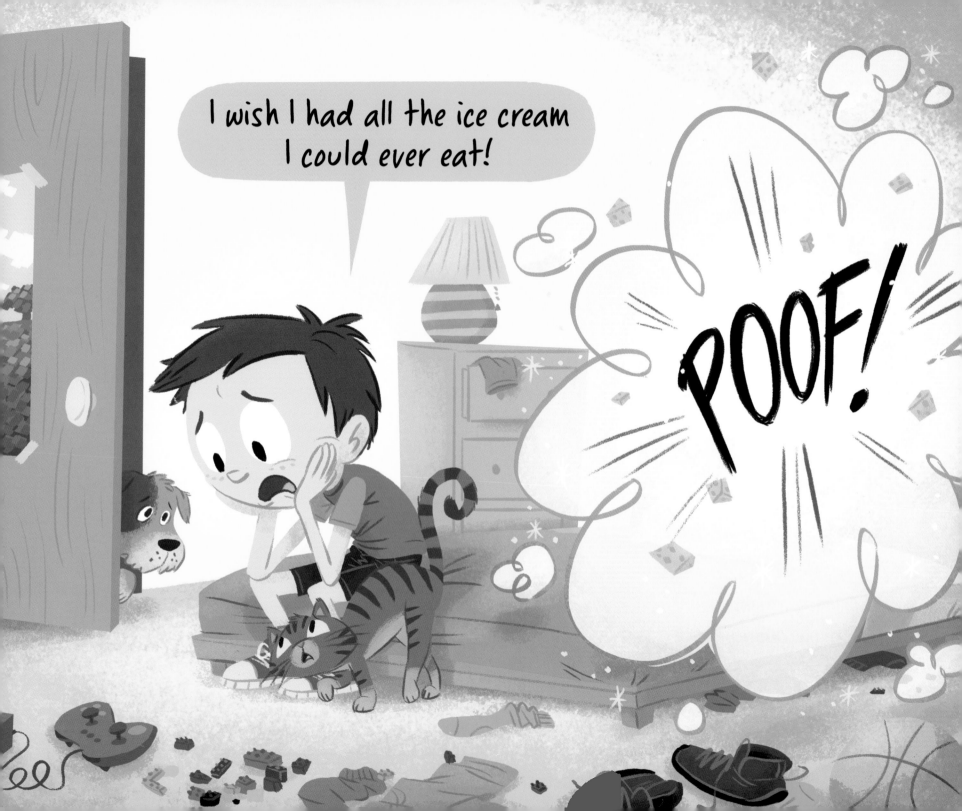

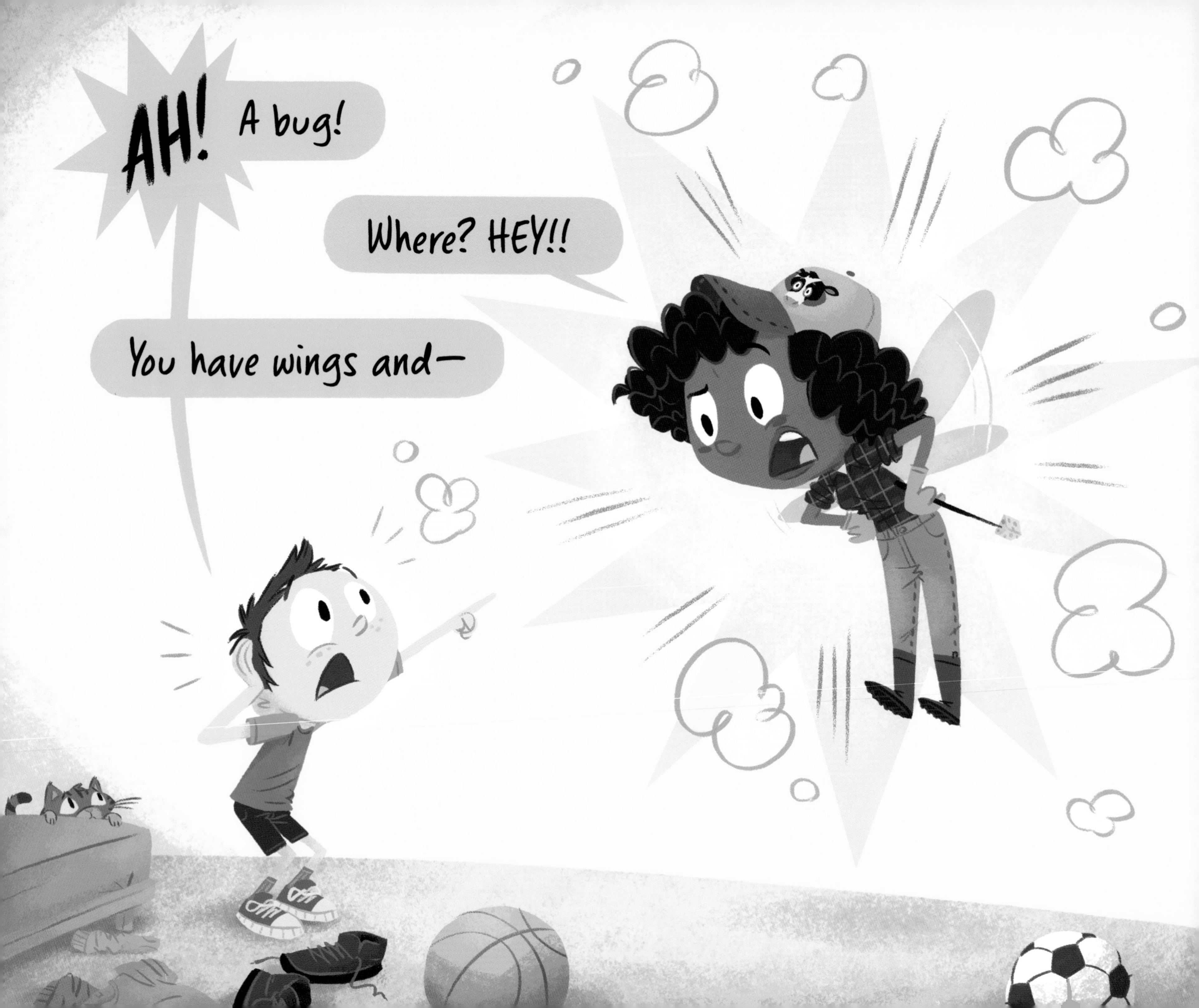
AH! A bug!
Where? HEY!!
You have wings and—

Cows need to be milked two or three times a day every day. Even on weekends and holidays.

Later...

Wow, making ice cream is a lot of work.

It certainly is.

Photo by Philip Gerlach, AFBFA

Do you want to meet a real dairy farmer named Chuck?
Visit www.feedingmindspress.com to watch a video of a real
dairy farmer doing his chores and making ice cream!

For free educational activities that accompany
this book visit: www.feedingmindspress.com.

The goal of FEEDING MINDS PRESS is to create and
publish accurate and engaging books about agriculture.

Make ice cream at home!

Be sure to have an adult help you whenever you're preparing or cooking food.

Materials needed:

- 1/4 cup sugar
- 1/2 tsp vanilla extract
- 1 cup milk
- 1 cup whipping cream
- 1 cup rock salt (Rock salt has larger grains of salt than table salt and works best for this recipe)

- 1 quart-size freezer plastic bag
- 1 gallon-size freezer plastic bag
- Duct Tape (length of a gallon-size freezer bag zipper)
- Towel
- Crushed ice or ice cubes, enough to fill the gallon bag

Instructions:

1. Put milk, whipping cream, sugar, and vanilla extract in the quart- size freezer bag.
2. Zip/seal the bag and fold the piece of duct tape over the zipper/seal so the ingredients won't leak out.
3. Place the bag of ingredients inside the gallon-size freezer bag.
4. Pack the gallon-size freezer bag with crushed ice so the ice surrounds the bag of ingredients.
5. Pour the rock salt evenly over the ice.
6. Wrap the bag in a towel.
7. Shake vigorously for 10 minutes.
8. Open the outer bag. Remove the inner bag with the ingredients. Wipe off the bag to remove any remaining ice, salt, and saltwater.
9. Cut the top off the bag and spoon the ice cream into cups. Enjoy!

Why salt? Science!

Ice cream freezes at -6 degrees C (21 degrees F). Ice cream can be made in a bag because the freezing point of water is actually lowered by adding rock salt to the ice between the bag walls. Heat energy is transferred easily from the milk through the plastic bag to the salty ice water causing the ice to melt. As it does so, the water in the milk freezes, resulting in ice cream!

Still hungry for more information?

Look for Right This Very Minute:
a table-to-farm book about food
and farming by Lisl Detlefsen and
Renée Kurilla to explore how more foods
make it from the farm to your plate.

Get the book and
related activities at
www.feedingmindspress.com.

Check out www.myamericanfarm.org for free online
games about where food comes from.

Visit www.agfoundation.org for fun blog posts, activities,
and even more farm fun!